Winnie the Pooh

my first ★ Bedtime storybook

 PRESS

Los Angeles • New York

Illustrated by the Disney Storybook Art Team
Based on the "Winnie the Pooh" works, by A. A. Milne and E. H. Shepard.

First Hardcover Edition, September 2021
10 9 8 7 6 5 4 3 2
ISBN 978-1-368-07237-3

FAC-025393-22010

Library of Congress Control Number: 2020947677
Printed in China

For more Disney Press fun, visit www.disneybooks.com

Contents

This book belongs to:

_____

Don't Be
Roo-diculous

One sunny afternoon, Roo and Tigger were BOUNCING together in the Hundred-Acre Wood.

Roo wanted to see who could bounce the highest. He scrunched up his face and closed his eyes and pushed off the ground as hard as he could.

Roo bounced himself into a flower bed.

"What's the matter, little buddy?" Tigger asked as he helped Roo up.

"I wish I could bounce as high as you," Roo said.

"Don't be ROO-DICULOUS," Tigger said. "You bounce pretty high for a little fella."

Roo sighed. "I wish I weren't so small," he said, looking up at the tree. "I want to swing from that branch."

Pooh was walking by and overheard.

"PERHAPS I CAN HELP," Pooh said. He held Roo up and stood on his tippy-toes. Roo reached as far as he could, and he got it!

"Whee!" Roo cried as he swung from the branch.

Pooh sat down beside the tree trunk. "Let me know when you're ready to come down."

But soon Pooh fell asleep. Roo didn't want to wake Pooh up, but his arms were getting tired, so he climbed up onto the branch. Roo was GETTING BORED.

After what seemed like a
long time, Roo heard someone
coming. It was Christopher Robin.

"I can help you down," said
Christopher Robin, who didn't
want to wake Pooh, either.
He held out his arms, and Roo
JUMPED right into them.

Once back on the
ground, Roo thanked
Christopher Robin.

Then he unhappily
headed home.

The next day, Kanga said she was going to make **APPLE PIE**. Roo tried his hardest, but he couldn't reach the apples.

Just then, Rabbit came along and asked what Roo was doing.

"I was trying to pick some apples for my mother."

"Why didn't you say so?" Rabbit said. He used his rake to knock down a bunch of apples.

Roo gave the apples to Kanga and then went for a long walk. He ended up at Eeyore's house of sticks.

As Roo looked at the sticks, he got an idea!

He borrowed Rabbit's hammer and some nails.
Then he went and collected some sticks.

Roo began to nail the sticks to a very tall tree.
Before long, he had a LADDER!

Roo couldn't help feeling proud of himself.

He climbed the tree using the ladder and SWUNG FROM THE BRANCHES.

Suddenly, Roo heard his mother and his friends looking for him.

"I'm up here!" he shouted.

"How on earth did you get up there?" Kanga asked. Roo pointed down at his ladder, then grinned from ear to ear as he climbed down it.

"I'm so proud of you, dear," Kanga said.
"You **DIDN'T GIVE UP.**" She lifted a tired
little Roo and tucked him into her pouch.

One bright and cheery day in the Hundred-Acre Wood, a mama duck watched her eggs hatch. Then she led her ducklings to the pond.

But Mama Duck didn't notice one SPOTTED EGG was left behind.

Winnie the Pooh and Piglet were taking a walk in the woods. They heard something chirping.

Pooh parted some lilies and saw a little duckling. "We must find his mother!" Pooh said. The two friends went off to search, but there were no ducks in sight.

"There's only one thing left to do," Pooh said. "We shall take him to my house."

They decided to call the duckling LITTLE.

At Pooh's house, they found a small box and made a comfy bed for Little. Then Piglet filled a small bowl with water and put it by his bed.

"Just in case he gets thirsty," Piglet said.

The next morning, Pooh, Piglet, and Little went to Rabbit's house for their first meal of the day.

Rabbit presented Little with a plate of GREEN BEANS, PEAS, and half of a chopped TOMATO.

After breakfast, Pooh and Piglet gave Little a bath. Then they headed home and stopped at OWL'S on the way.

"Let me show you how to primp and plump those fuzzy yellow feathers of yours," Owl said.

Once they said good-bye to Owl, a fuller, fluffier Little waddled home with Winnie the Pooh.

The very next day, Tigger and Roo came to give Little a BOUNCING LESSON.

"Let's bounce to the pond and go for a swim!" Tigger cried.

At the pond, Roo introduced Little to the most AMAZING creatures.

The next day, Eeyore came by to teach Little how
to WADDLE.

Little and Eeyore waddled around the thistle patch.

Eeyore tried to walk Little to Pooh's house, but he got lost.

"Better just sit tight and wait for somebody to come and find us," Eeyore said. Before long, they had both fallen ASLEEP. Pooh and Piglet found them fast asleep underneath a willow tree.

Together, the friends made it back to Pooh's house. When Pooh and Piglet put Little to bed, they heard him QUACKING.

"Listen, Pooh," Piglet said. "I think he's missing his mama."

"Oh, dear. Perhaps it's time to try to find his mother again."

The next day, Pooh and Piglet, along with Kanga and Roo, took Little back to the pond. They found MAMA DUCK!

There was lots of hugging and clapping, and both Mama Duck and Little looked very happy.

"I will miss Little," Pooh said to his friends. "But I'm happy he's going to be with his family now."

The Forgiving Friend

It was a beautiful sunny day. Pooh went to visit Rabbit and found him PICKING VEGETABLES from his garden.

Pooh thought his other friends should help, so he went to get them.

After Pooh gathered
the rest of his friends,
he and Piglet went
to Kanga's house to
check on a sick Roo.

Roo wanted some of Kanga's VEGETABLE SOUP.
"She doesn't have any vegetables, so she can't make
it," Roo explained to his friends.

Piglet told Pooh he
would be right back.
He went to Rabbit's house
for vegetables, but he
couldn't find Rabbit.
He knew Rabbit wouldn't
mind, so he took what
he needed.

Piglet hurried
back to Kanga's house,
but Pooh was already
gone. Piglet stayed
to HELP MAKE
THE SOUP.

Later, when the rest of the friends got to Rabbit's garden, they saw the vegetables had been picked already.

Tigger was VERY SUSPICIOUS. He was going to get to the bottom of this mystery.

First Tigger approached Rabbit. "Don't be ridiculous," Rabbit said. "Why would I take my own vegetables?"

Rabbit shooed Tigger away, and he went on with his search.

Tigger questioned all his friends, but he learned nothing. Then he went to see his buddy Roo.

When he got there, he saw that KANGA HAD COOKED UP A STORM. "Did all these vegetables come from your garden?" Tigger asked.

"Why, no, Tigger," she said. "Piglet brought them from Rabbit's garden."

AHA! The case of the missing "vegerritables" was solved.

"I knew it all along!" cried Tigger. "I've got to go tell ol' Long Ears! Be back in a jifferoo."

Tigger bounded FAST AND FURIOUSLY to Rabbit's house. When he told him the answer to the mystery, Rabbit was not pleased.

"Piglet should have asked before taking my vegetables," said Rabbit. "AND I PLAN TO TELL HIM SO!"

Tigger and Rabbit found Piglet at Pooh's house.

"I wanted to ask you first, Rabbit," Piglet began, "but you weren't home. Here, take these haycorn muffins as an 'I'M SORRY' GIFT."

Rabbit softened after listening to Piglet. "I forgive you, Piglet."

Then he looked at Piglet's basket. "Why don't we take your muffins and the last of my vegetables over to Kanga and Roo right now?"

At Roo's house, Rabbit and Piglet presented their gifts.

"I hope you're planning to stay for dinner," said Kanga.

"This forgiveness business looks pretty tasty," said Tigger.

"LET'S EAT!" said Pooh.

Pooh's Kindness Game

One morning, Eeyore was in the THISTLE PATCH and ran into a big rock. When he tried to move it, he knocked over a pile of rocks and one fell on his tail. He was stuck.

Piglet found Eeyore and tried to help him, but Piglet couldn't move the rock alone.

Piglet left and came back with help. "Don't worry,"
Rabbit said. "WE'LL THINK OF SOMETHING."

"I know," Piglet said. "If we all work together to
push it, we can move the rock."

So Pooh, Piglet, Tigger, and
Rabbit pushed until the rock
rolled away.

Eeyore could not have
been more GRATEFUL for
their help. "Thanks," he said.
"That certainly does feel better."

Everyone was so
pleased. It gave Pooh
an idea. Why not play a
KINDNESS GAME,
where everyone does a
good deed for the next
five days.

The next day, as Pooh was cleaning, he found a basket that would be perfect for Piglet's haycorns.

Piglet was delighted. It was the PERFECT GIFT.

On the second day, Rabbit made a special
HONEY delivery to Pooh. And on the third day,
Tigger helped Rabbit in his GARDEN.

On the fourth day, Piglet took HAYCORN MUFFINS to Kanga and Roo.

On the fifth day, Eeyore kept Tigger COMPANY when no one else was around.

On the sixth day, Pooh and his friends came
together to talk about all they had done over the
previous five days.

Everyone was in a particularly good mood.

Pooh said, "It must be the kindness game!"

Pooh and his friends learned a very important

lesson: when you do something for someone else,

not only does it make that someone feel happy . . .

but IT MAKES YOU FEEL HAPPY, TOO!

The Sweetest Friends

"Good morning, Piglet," Pooh said.

"Good morning, Pooh," Piglet said.

It was a sunny day in the Hundred-Acre Wood. Piglet had made haycorn pie, and Pooh had brought honey.

After they ate, Piglet wanted to TAKE A WALK.

Pooh yawned and stretched. "Lead the way, Piglet." They decided to pay Eeyore a visit.

"It's a lovely summer day," Piglet said. Eeyore shrugged.

When they left Eeyore's house, Pooh was hungry.

"I believe we need something to eat," he said, patting his tummy. "Perhaps some honey."

Just then, a bee flew by. Pooh and his tummy followed it.

Piglet saw a BEAUTIFUL BUTTERFLY and followed it in the opposite direction of the bee.

"Would you like to look at the butterfly with my binoculars, Pooh?" Piglet asked, without looking behind him.

When there was no answer, Piglet turned toward the tree where Pooh liked to nap, but he was not napping there. Piglet hurried off to find his friend.

Meanwhile, Pooh had finished his encounter with the bee—or rather bees—and was having similar thoughts about Piglet.

Buzz
Buzz
Buzz

Buzzzz

Not at all sure how he had wound up without Piglet
or honey, Pooh resolved to find one first and then
the other.

Eventually, Pooh found Piglet sitting on a log. The two friends were VERY HAPPY TO HAVE FOUND EACH OTHER.

"I will make sure to say GOOD-BYE next time I leave you," said Piglet, smiling as he realized there would be a next time.

"And I shall, as well," Pooh replied.

"What would you like to do tomorrow?" Piglet asked.

"Perhaps we can meet for breakfast?" Pooh replied.

"And then maybe we can take a walk," said Piglet.

"Wonderful!" said Pooh.

What Good Friends Do

One night in the Hundred-Acre Wood, a nervous Piglet could not sleep.

"Oh, d-d-d-dear," Piglet said. "I better just stay here until morning, keeping watch for HEFFALUMPS, WOOZLES, and all other creatures that come out at night!"

The next day, Pooh came to Piglet's room. Piglet asked if he could hear something. All Pooh could hear was the birds.

"Not the birds, Pooh," said Piglet. "It's the woozles and the heffalumps that set their traps inside my house!"

"I don't see anyone in here except you and me, Piglet," said Pooh.

"But they kept me up all night," Piglet said. Pooh looked around the house, but he didn't find anything.

Soon Rabbit stopped by. Just then, a CLANGING and BANGING began, sending Piglet beneath a chair.

"It sounds like your pipes need tightening. I can fix that!" Rabbit said, and he got to work.

Piglet was getting nervous again. Pooh turned to his friend. "What if you PRETEND TO BE BRAVE? Perhaps you might get so busy pretending to be brave that you forget that you're pretending. And then you can go on being brave." Pooh spent the rest of the day at Piglet's.

In the morning, Pooh awoke to find Piglet outside waving a broom in the air.

"LOOK, POOH! I'm shooing these blackbirds away. They've been cawing and screeching at me. But thanks to my trusty broom, I feel brave!"

Pooh suggested they take a walk. "When you see there's nothing scary out there, it might help you feel brave."

Piglet stopped to admire a butterfly. Then he noticed he was alone. He heard a strange humming and he got nervous. "BE BRAVE, BE BRAVE, BE BRAVE," he said to himself.

Piglet walked on bravely, looking for Pooh. "Pooh . . . is that you?" Piglet asked.

"Yes, it's me, Piglet," Pooh said. "The leaves are quite loud today. But look how brave you were!"

Pooh **HUGGED** his friend.

"I couldn't have done it without you believing in me, Pooh. That helped me believe in myself," Piglet said.

"Well," Pooh said, "THAT'S JUST WHAT GOOD FRIENDS DO."